THE
GOOD·FOR·SOMETHING
DRAGON

THE
GOOD·FOR·SOMETHING
DRAGON

by Judith Ross Enderle & Stephanie Gordon Tessler

illustrated by Les Gray

Boyds Mills Press

Published by Caroline House
Boyds Mills Press, Inc.
A Highlights Company
815 Church Street
Honesdale, Pennsylvania 18431
Printed in Mexico

Publisher Cataloging-in-Publication Data
Enderle, Judith Ross.
    The good-for-something dragon / by Judith Ross Enderle and Stephanie
Gordon Tessler ; illustrated by Les Gray.—1st ed.
[32]p. : col. ill. ; cm.
Summary: A young boy must prove to his father why a little dragon is worth
keeping in the castle.
ISBN 1-56397-214-X
1. Dragons—Juvenile fiction. [1. Dragons—Fiction.]
I. Tessler, Stephanie Gordon. II. Gray, Les, ill. III. Title.
    [E]—dc20   1993
Library of Congress Catalog Card Number: 92-75859   CIP AC

First edition, 1993
Book designed by Les Gray
The text of this book is set in 16-point Century Old Style.
The illustrations are done in watercolors.
Distributed by St. Martin's Press

10 9 8 7 6 5 4 3 2

For Panda, our office dragon,
and in memory of Duffie and Patches
for all of your wonderful wet kisses!

–J.R.E. & S.G.T.

For Jackie

–L.G.

James stood before Sir Simon in the great hall. "May I keep him, Father?" he asked.

Sir Simon the Giant-Catcher peered over his news scroll. "Dragons, no matter how small, do not belong in a castle," he said.

James rested his chin on the baby dragon's head. "But Ashley is special, Father."

"And how is he different from other dragons?" asked Sir Simon.

James thought and thought. But he couldn't think of one different thing, though he knew there must be one hundred. There just had to be!

Ashley licked James on the tip of his freckled nose.

"Please, fifty trillion times," James pleaded.

His father shook his head. "Ashley is just a good-for-nothing dragon."

James sighed his saddest sigh as Sir Simon took his shield from the hook by the door. "In three days, I set out to catch a gallivanting giant who is bounding about our kingdom doing damage. You have until I leave to prove your dragon is good for something."

"Thank you, Father! Did you hear that, Ashley?" James did a little dance, and Ashley licked James's face.

Then, with the baby dragon in his arms, James ran down the stone steps to the kitchen, where delicious scents of boar broth and kidney pie tickled his nose. And where Cook pointed at Ashley with her spoon and shouted, "Is that a dragon?"

"My very own dragon." James poked a finger in the kidney pie. "But Father says Ashley must be good for something or I can't keep him."

Cook shooed him away from the table. "Dragons dash about distressing cooks and damsels. Dragons are good-for-nothing."

"My dragon is special." James put Ashley on the floor. "Make a flame for Cook," he said.

The little dragon's flame swirled around the soup pot in the fireplace until boar broth bubbled onto the hot coals.

Cook waved her spoon like a mighty sword. "Shoo! Scat! He's making a mess! Good-for-nothing dragon!"

Ears back, tail down, the little dragon flew into James's arms. He licked James's face as they ran.

The next morning, James took Ashley to the stables. The horses stamped and snorted in their stalls, and the stableman threw down his pitchfork. "Ho, young sir! What have you there?" he called.

"It's my baby dragon. He'll help you guard the horses," said James.

The stableman marched toward him like the captain of the guard. "Horses and dragons? Never! Now get that good-for-nothing dragon out of my stable."

So James shuffled back to the castle, while Ashley flew around and around James's head and licked James's face. "You are good for something," James said. But he thought and thought. And he could not think of one good thing, though he knew there must be five hundred. There just had to be!

At dinner, Sir Simon looked stormy. "I heard from Cook and from the stableman about your good-for-nothing dragon," he said.

James looked at his plate.

Sir Simon sat back. "Only one more day, son. But you cannot change the nature of things—not in a hundred days."

James folded his arms. "Ashley is special, Father."

Sir Simon sighed. He cut into his kidney pie. And Ashley crept beneath the table.

James knew the pie was very tasty, but he just wasn't hungry. He slipped a fat lardoon to Ashley. Hiccup! went the little dragon.

Seconds later, Sir Simon leaped from his chair. He fanned his kneecaps. "A dragon, no matter how small, does not belong in a castle," he roared. "And he most certainly does not belong under the dining room table."

"Excuse us, please!" James cried, and he and Ashley sped up the tower stairs.

"And dragons, no matter how small, are good-for-nothing," Sir Simon shouted after them.

In his room, James sat in the middle of his bed. "Father is very angry," he said. Ashley's dragon eyes were sad. His dragon wings were woeful. His dragon tail drooped. He licked James's face.

"You must be good for something," said James. He thought and thought. But he could not think of one thing, though he knew there must be a thousand. There just had to be! Finally, he drifted off to sleep.

Before dawn, a great shudder rumbled through the castle, sending mice scurrying and dust sifting from ancient crevices. James jumped out of bed, and Ashley flew to the door. Puffs of dragon smoke ringed the room. Together they sped down the tower stairs.

In the great hall, Cook dashed about. "Save us! Save us!" she cried.

"Open the great door," Sir Simon commanded as he lifted his shield from the hook.

Bravely, James threw the bolt.
A fierce giant loomed in the glow of the torchlights. He rattled the courtyard gate. The latch clanked. The hinges groaned. "LET ME IN!" he roared. "Give me your bag of baubles. Give me your harp that hums. And your pig that lays the golden eggs." The giant rumbled and thundered. He stomped and threatened.

Sir Simon shouted back, "I have no bag of baubles. There is no harp that hums here. And my pigs do not lay eggs, golden or otherwise. I am Sir Simon, the famous giant-catcher. So begone!"

"WHO?" the giant roared.

"If you won't be gone, you shall be locked away for a hundred hundred years." Sir Simon raised his shield and rushed the giant at the gate.

"Never! Give me baubles, harps, and pigs," demanded the giant. And he kicked the gate so hard that his big toe crashed through, bumping Sir Simon, who clattered to the ground.

James raced to his father's side, while Ashley darted back and forth. Puff! Puff! Puff! Out billowed clouds of smoke larger than the little dragon.

The giant rattled the gate like a ferocious windstorm. "I'm coming in NOW," he roared.

Up, up, up soared the little dragon. He circled the giant's head. He licked the giant's nose.

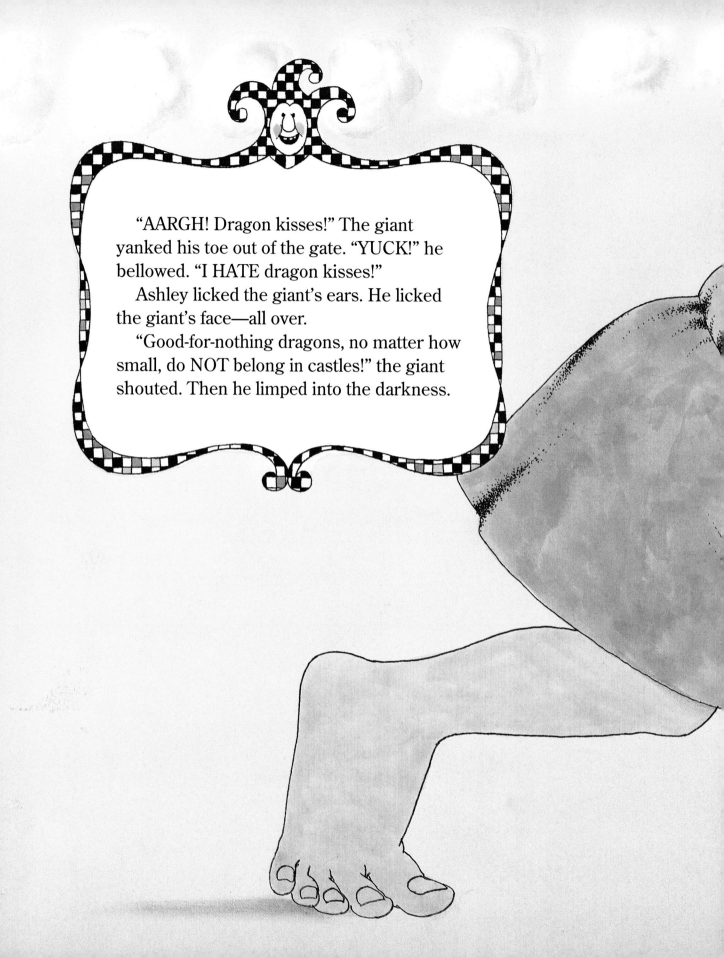

"AARGH! Dragon kisses!" The giant yanked his toe out of the gate. "YUCK!" he bellowed. "I HATE dragon kisses!"

Ashley licked the giant's ears. He licked the giant's face—all over.

"Good-for-nothing dragons, no matter how small, do NOT belong in castles!" the giant shouted. Then he limped into the darkness.

The next morning, the sign on the courtyard gate said: BEWARE OF THE DRAGON.